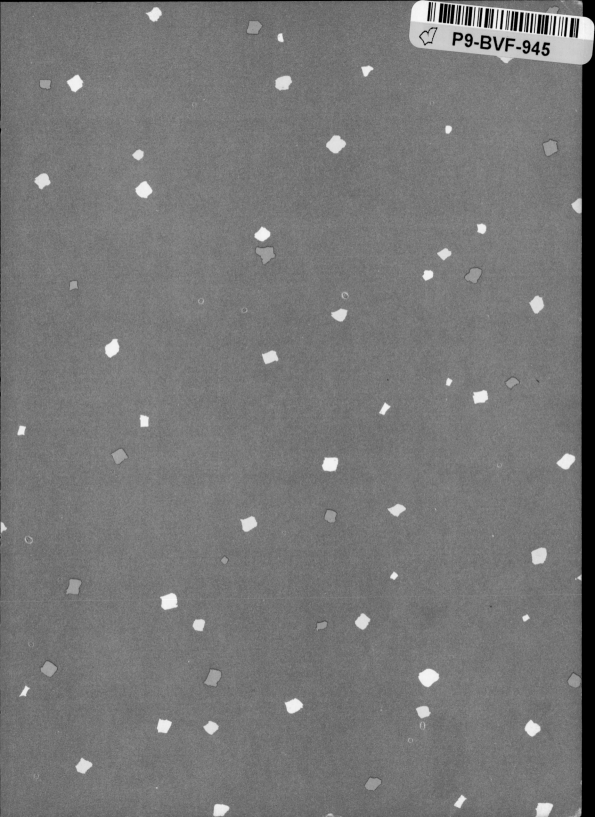

THE Clown-Arounds

Library of Congress Cataloging in Publication Data.
Cole, Joanna.   The Clown-Arounds.
SUMMARY: The Clown-Around family enters a contest
which promises a big surprise to the winner.
|1.   Clowns—Fiction.   2.   Humorous stories|
I.   Smath, Jerry.   II.   Title.
PZ7.C67346C1 |E| 81-4662
ISBN 0-8193-1059-X AACR2 ISBN 0-8193-1060-3 (lib. bdg.)

THE Clown-Arounds

by Joanna Cole

pictures by Jerry Smath

Parents Magazine Press
New York

A Parents Magazine   READ ALOUD AND EASY READING PROGRAM® Selection.

The Clown-Around family lives in
an ordinary town on an ordinary street.
But the Clown-Arounds are not an
ordinary family.

Can you tell which house belongs
to the Clown-Arounds? That's *right*!
They live in house number nine. How
did you guess?

Here is the whole Clown-Around family still asleep in their beds.

There is Mr. Clown-Around,

Mrs. Clown-Around,

their daughter, Bubbles,

the Baby,

and Wag-Around, their dog.

In the morning, when their alarm clock goes off, the Clown-Arounds leap out of bed happily, ready to start a new day.

Bubbles takes a morning bath,

but Baby and Wag-Around prefer a shower.

Meals are a lot of fun at the Clown-Arounds' house.

They always have pie — even
for breakfast!

Whenever Mr. Clown-Around leaves the house, the whole family comes out to wave good-bye.

While Mrs. Clown-Around
does some housework,

Baby, Bubbles and Wag-Around
play out in the yard.

Later in the day, the Clown-Arounds
like to take a walk in the park ...

or go for a swim at the beach.
It's fun to be a Clown-Around!

One day, the Clown-Arounds found a letter in their mailbox.

It said:

Dear Family,

Why not have
some fun?
Enter this contest.
Just send a
family photo.
Maybe you'll win
"THE BIG SURPRISE."

The Clown-Arounds wanted to have fun.
They wanted to win The Big Surprise.

So they looked through their photo album.
Finally they found just the right picture
and mailed it in to the contest.

The next day, they looked in the
mailbox. But The Big Surprise had not
come by mail.

The following day, they waited by
the telephone. But no one called about
The Big Surprise.

The Clown-Arounds felt sad. Maybe
someone else had won the contest.

They tried to cheer each other up,

but nothing helped.

They were still sad.

Then a truck rolled down the
street. The Big Surprise was being
delivered right to their doorstep.

What a surprise! It was just right
for the Clown-Arounds! Now they could
really go places.

And their favorite place to go
is the circus.

Because the Clown-Arounds think
the circus is more fun than anything.
Don't you?

About the Author

JOANNA COLE was an elementary school teacher and a children's book editor before becoming a full-time children's book author. *The Clown-Arounds* is the first story she has written for Parents.

Ms. Cole lives with her husband and their four year old daughter in New York City.

About the Artist

JERRY SMATH worked in films for many years before he turned to illustration for children's magazines and books. He has written and illustrated two previous books for Parents — *But No Elephants* and *The Housekeeper's Dog*.

Mr. Smath lives with his wife, Valerie, and their two dogs in Westchester County, New York.

Both Joanna Cole and Jerry Smath admit that they are secret Clown-Arounds at heart. How about *you*?